How to be a hero

This book is not like others you may have read. You are the hero of this adventure. It is up to you to make decisions that will affect how the adventure unfolds.

Each section of this book is numbered. At the end of most sections, you will have to make a choice. The choice you make will take you to a different section of the book.

Some of your choices will help you to complete the adventure successfully. But choose carefully, some of your decisions could be fatal!

If you fail, then start the adventure again and learn from your mistake.

If you choose correctly you will succeed in your mission.

Don't be a zero, be a hero!

The quest so far...

You are a member of a Special Forces naval unit. You are an expert diver and can pilot submarines of all types. You are a specialist in underwater combat and have taken part in many dangerous missions in all of the world's oceans. Your bravery and skill have won you many medals.

You have been recruited by Admiral Crabbe, leader of ORCA — the Ocean Research Central Agency — a top-secret unit whose mission is to patrol the planet's oceans and deal with any threats to humankind from hostile creatures of the deep. Your quest is to help fight the Atlanteans, a race of amphibians who are determined to destroy humankind.

To help you in your quest you have been given command of the Barracuda, the most advanced submarine in the world. The Mer, another amphibian race, created this amazing machine. The Mer are sworn enemies of the Atlanteans and have an alliance with humankind.

TOP SECRET: ORCA Barracuda

(1) Stunfish launcher –
self-propelled weapons resembling
sunfish that produce a low-frequency
sonic wave to knock out enemy
defences.

(2) Crew cockpit –
where the Barracuda
pilots sit.

(3) Countermeasures –
ultra-fast mini-rockets that
target and destroy enemy
torpedoes.

(4) Water cannon –
fires a super-heated water
jet at close range, which
is hot enough to cut
through metal.

(5) Torpedo tubes –
launch supercavitation
torpedoes with
explosive warheads.

**(6) Sub-aqua
bike bays –**
pods for launching
the sub-aqua bikes.

(7) Propulsion system –
powers the sub through the water.
Also capable of a short 'jet boost'.

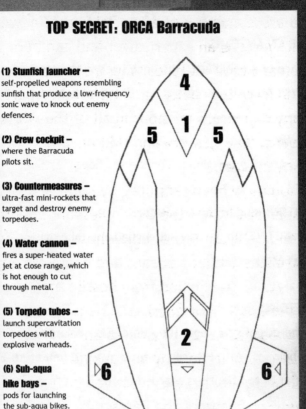

THE ATLANTEANS:

A race of amphibians, who once lived in the legendary city of Atlantis. Masters of sea-based technology.

HOME:

New Atlantis, a realm under the sea floor.

TRITON: King of the Atlanteans

OBJECTIVE: To destroy humankind and take over the Earth.

HISTORY:

Hundreds of years ago, the Atlanteans declared war on humans. With the Mer's help they were defeated. Entrance to Atlantis is guarded by the Mer.

BACKGROUND INFORMATION:

The Atlanteans have broken out from New Atlantis. They have declared war on humans and the Mer.

With the help of Shen, a female Mer, you have managed to defeat Hydros, one of Triton's commanders. You stopped his forces from capturing a top-secret island base and getting hold of the missiles stored there. You also managed to salvage the pressure shield generator from Hydros's command ship. Shen has fitted this to the Barracuda, which means it can dive to unlimited depths. You are now preparing to hunt down the Atlanteans and send them back to their realm under the sea before they can carry out Triton's threats to destroy humankind.

The future of the Earth depends on you... Go to 1.

1

You and Shen are taking the Barracuda for a test dive to see how well the captured pressure shield generator works. You have already reached a depth of 10,000 metres.

"To get to this depth without any problems is extraordinary," you say. "This shield is incredible."

Shen nods. "We will need it if we are going to find the hole in the seabed where the Atlanteans broke out."

Before you can reply, an alarm begins to wail. "Warning! Crush depth exceeded! Outside pressure too great," warns the Barracuda.

"We'd better return to the surface," you say.

Shen shakes her head. "Don't worry, I didn't have time to re-program the Barracuda's warning systems when I fitted the shield generator. We're safe."

"Are you sure?" you ask.

"I said we're safe," she replies. "Don't you trust me?"

To return to the surface, go to 36.
If you trust Shen, go to 17.

2

"An all-out attack is impossible," you say.
"The cyborg's defensive shield is too strong.
We'll have to neutralise it. That means getting
inside the ship. I'll take a sub-aqua bike over
there while you take the Barracuda out of
range and contact ORCA. You've got to send
them our location."

"Right. It's lucky that our engineers were able
to make smaller copies of the pressure shield
generator to protect us and our aquabikes."

Shen begins to prepare the bike as you put
on your aquasuit.

To set off immediately, go to 23.

**If you want to find out more about the
Man-of-war, go to 45.**

3

"We're outnumbered, we have to get out
of here! Switch to jet boost," you order.
But before the Barracuda can obey, a huge
explosion rocks the super sub.

"Hull breached!" warns Shen.

Another torpedeo hits.

"The pressure shield generator is failing!"

It's the last thing you hear as the outside water pressure crushes the Barracuda, sending you into the darkness.

You have failed. To begin your mission again, go to 1.

4

"There are too many enemy ships to take on," you say to Shen.

She nods in agreement. "Let's stay in stealth mode and follow the ship."

As the Man-of-war moves away, you follow it

at a distance.

After several hours, the Man-of-war slows down and stops.

"Where are we?" you ask.

"We're off the east coast of China," replies Shen. "We're within range of Chinese, Korean and Russian nuclear bases."

"If the Atlanteans attack, each country will blame the other. The Atlanteans will start a new world war!" you say grimly.

"We have to tell ORCA," says Shen.

"If we do we'll have to break from stealth mode," you reply. "We'll give away our position."

If you want to contact ORCA now, go to 31.

If you want to stay in stealth mode, go to 49.

5

You accelerate and just manage to squeeze through the closing gap.

As you shoot out of the Man-of-war, you see the ocean lit up by explosions as the ORCA defence subs and the Atlantean ships do battle.

"Harvester missiles being launched in thirty seconds," warns Shen. "I'm nearly at your position."

You speed towards your parked sub-aqua bike and transfer from the seahorse, taking the defensive shield with you. Suddenly there is a massive explosion as the harvester anti-submarine missiles strike the Man-of-war. The huge ship erupts, sending a shockwave through

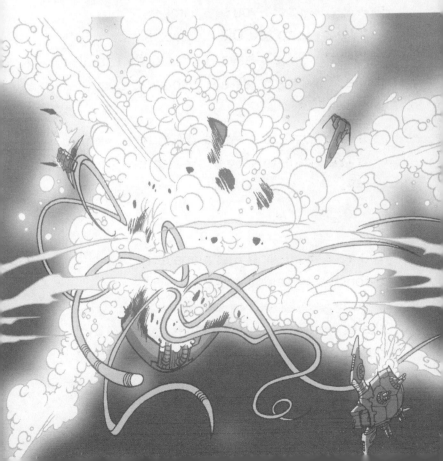

the water, scattering many Atlantean vessels
and knocking you from your bike.

"Well, I'm still in one piece!" you tell Shen.
At that moment you see a lone figure riding
towards you on the back of a huge white cyborg

shark. You realise that this is Hadal. He must have escaped from the Man-of-war!

He closes in on you and the shark's mouth opens, revealing two deadly looking guns.

To get back on your sub-aqua bike, go to 12.

To fight the Atlantean commander, go to 37.

To ask Shen for help, go to 19.

6

"Those ships need to be dealt with," you decide. "Lock on and fire torpedoes."

Seconds later the Turtle troopships are destroyed.

Shen shakes her head. "I think we should have tracked them. They could have been useful to us."

You shrug. "Too late now. Let's get back to ORCA HQ, re-arm the Barracuda and see what Admiral Crabbe has lined up for us."

Go to 33.

7

You hit the throttle, but the Atlanteans follow on their mounts, sending a volley of metal lassos towards you. You try to avoid them, but one wraps itself around your body. You are pulled from the bike and float in the water. An Atlantean moves in and jabs you with an electro-lance. You feel a mind-numbing pain and then pass into blackness.

Go to 43.

8

"We're close enough for a surprise attack on the ship," you say. "We fire our stunfish to knock out the defences and follow up with torpedoes. That should crack open the hull. Then we tell ORCA where we are, and they can come and mop up the rest of the Atlanteans." Shen shrugs and agrees.

You target and fire the stunfish at the cyborg. They hit the hull.

"Fire torpedoes!" you order.

The torpedoes speed towards the Man-of-war, but before they can strike home, the ship's defences take out the torpedoes!

"The stunfish didn't work," cries Shen.

The Barracuda's alarms sound. "Incoming

torpedoes launched! Impact 10 seconds!"

"Launching countermeasures," says Shen.

"Evasive action!" you order, but it is too late. The Barracuda is hit.

The explosion is the last thing you hear as more torpedoes hit and blow the Barracuda apart.

Go back to 1 to try again.

9

"Let's see if there are any more vessels," you say. "Scan again on all devices: thermal, sonar and radar."

The Barracuda obeys and seconds later projects an image of two Lionfish destroyers.

"There you are," you whisper.

"Enemy destroyers at 70 degrees and five hundred metres away, but closing in," reports Shen.

To attack the destroyers, go to 30.
To attack the troopships, go to 48.
If you wish to retreat, go to 40.

10

You punch up the seahorse's map system and find the engine room. You leave your seahorse on the other side of the airlock, and make your way through the corridors. The aquasuit's visor screen flashes up a warning, "ORCA attack in 20 minutes." You increase speed and soon reach the engine room.

The door is guarded by two Atlantean warriors. Before they can react, you take them out with a burst from your jet gun and then blast open the doors with a self-propelled grenade.

You move inside.

The engine room is full of Atlantean engineers. They are shocked to see you!

In front of you is a control panel, with the defensive shield unit!

If you decide to attack the engineers, go to 29.

If you want to walk over to the defensive shield control panel, go to 47.

11

The Barracuda heads towards the Atlantean forces at jet boost speed. It is not long before you find yourself just outside the detection range of their scanners.

The tracking devices on the Turtle troopships show there are hundreds of Atlantean ships gathering around the cyborg Man-of-war.

"They must be getting ready for an attack," you say. "If we can destroy the fleet, I reckon that we'll send the remaining ships back to Atlantis. Then we can follow them and find the hole on the ocean floor."

If you wish to attack the Atlantean force, go to 28.

If you wish to use stealth mode, go to 42.

12

You spin around, but before you can get away, the guns open fire. A cloud of deadly steel darts hammer into you, turning the water red.

You came so far, but have failed. To begin again, go back to 1.

13

"Good idea," you say. You press a button and two tracking devices are sent speeding on their way to the troopships.

The devices hit the metal hulls and attach themselves.

Shen checks the monitor. "Tracking devices activated. They could be very useful later," she says.

You nod. "I hope so. Let's get back to ORCA HQ, re-arm the Barracuda and see what Admiral Crabbe has lined up for us."

Go to 33.

14

You ride the sub-aqua bike towards the Man-of-war's hangar. The huge sub is covered in hundreds of searchlights that cut through the blackness of the water.

As you wonder how you will get into the hangar, you see two Atlantean guards on patrol. They are riding seahorses and both carry deadly electro-lances.

Suddenly, one of the beams of light swings around onto you! The Atlanteans see you and head towards you.

If you wish to attack the patrol, go to 27.

If you wish to try to escape, go to 7.

15

"It's a shame we destroyed the troopships," says Shen. "If we'd used a tracking device, maybe they would have led us to the Atlantean force."

"What do you mean?" asks Admiral Crabbe.

You tell him about destroying the ships.

"You fool!" explodes the admiral. "You should have tracked them!" He shakes his head. "I don't need a hothead like you. You're going back to your unit!"

Your quest is over. If you want to begin again, go to 1.

16

You decide to use the seahorse to get past the Man-of-war's ID scanning system. As you head towards the hangar entrance, you are caught in a blue light beam. You realise that you are being scanned.

You pass through the entry doors and breathe a sigh of relief. You were right to use the seahorse!

As you move through the hangar, your comms

link opens up. It is Shen. "ORCA's defence subs will be here within an hour," she tells you.

You know that you will have to find the defensive shield and disable it or the attack will fail.

If you want to head to the engine room, go to 10.

If you want to head to the control room, go to 32.

17

"I trust you," you say. "But can you do something about that alarm? The noise is driving me crazy."

Shen smiles and taps a button, and the alarm cuts off.

As the Barracuda heads deeper, you stare out of the window but can see very little. Even the Barracuda's powerful lights hardly pierce the blackness of the sea.

"The Atlanteans could be anywhere in this," you say. "No wonder it's taking time to find out where they broke through."

The Barracuda gives a warning. "Two slow moving objects ahead..."

An image projects onto a screen.

"Atlantean Turtle troopships! They don't seem to have spotted us," Shen says. "What should we do?"

If you wish to find out more about the troopships, go to 26.

If you wish to attack them immediately, go to 48.

18

"We have to stop the Man-of-war getting away!" you say. "Cancel stealth mode, we must attack."

You launch torpedoes and they shoot towards the Man-of-war. They hit, but explode harmlessly against the hull.

Immediately, the Barracuda's scanners detect enemy torpedoes heading towards you — you have given away your position! More torpedoes launch from the Man-of-war's tentacles.

"Deploy countermeasures!" you cry as you swing the super sub around.

You fight back and destroy several Atlantean

ships as they turn to attack. But more vessels close in.

To continue the fight, go to 35.
If you wish to retreat, go to 3.

19

"I need some help here," you tell Shen as Hadal opens fire with the shark's guns.

"Use the defensive shield," she says. You push the defensive shield panel into the chest armour of your aquasuit. You are shocked when it grows into the fabric! The shark gun's razor darts simply bounce off you like hail!

Hadal attacks again, but the darts cannot get through the defensive shield.

"The defensive shield works, Shen!" You jump onto your sub-aqua bike and launch six sea dart missiles at the cyborg shark. In turn, the shark fires explosive teeth at the missiles, destroying them all. Hadal moves in with his electro-lance, when suddenly you see bright lights heading towards you. It's the Barracuda!

"Hold on tight — this might sting a bit," warns Shen.

There is a burst of bubbles as she launches a torpedo. It zooms past you and hits Hadal head on! The force of the explosion sends you spinning and you black out.

Go to 50.

20

"Let's head to the meeting point and surprise them," you say.

"Don't be such a hothead," snaps Admiral Crabbe. "We need to find out more about the location, and to find out if there *is* a build-up of enemy forces. We need more intelligence."

You realise that the admiral is right.

Calm down and go to 24.

21

You raise you hands in surrender. The Atlanteans move in towards you.

An electro-lance is thrust into your body. You feel a surge of intense pain before passing into blackness.

Go to 43.

22

"Let's move it!" you shout. You spin the Barracuda away, and the incoming torpedoes miss.

However, the troopships open fire with their barnacle cannons, sending a salvo of explosive bombs your way.

"We can't avoid all of them," cries Shen. "We've got to attack the destroyers before we're blown apart!"

If you wish to take Shen's advice, go to 30. If you don't, go to 3.

23

You launch the sub-aqua bike and head for the Man-of-war, while Shen pilots the Barracuda out of range so she can contact ORCA safely.

Atlantean vessels surround the Man-of-war. You make your way through the water using the bike's NAV system. Your scanner picks up dozens of ships leaving the Man-of-war's main hangar.

If you wish to head towards the hangar entrance, go to 14.

If you wish to search for a different way in, go to 39.

24

"So how do we find out more about the location of the troopships?" you ask.

"We can use the visual imaging system on the tracking devices," suggests Shen.

The admiral nods approval. "Then do it."

Within minutes there is a 3-D image of the location. You gasp as a gigantic jellyfish is revealed. Hundreds of other smaller ships surround it.

"Is that for real?" you ask.

"It's a cyborg Man-of-war," replies Shen.

"The most powerful vessel in the Atlantean fleet. It must be Commander Hadal's mother ship."

"Looks like we've found the Atlantean's meeting point," says Admiral Crabbe. "We need to get our defence subs to that location as soon as possible. I'll contact the Mer people and tell them what's happening."

An hour later you and Shen are aboard the Barracuda, speeding towards the Atlantean forces.

If you wish to find out more about the cyborg Man-of-war, go to 38.

If you don't, go to 11.

25

You ignore the alarms and move forward towards the airlock. But before you get any further, the Atlantean guards surround you. They are armed with electro-lances. They signal you to stop.

To speed into the airlock, go to 7.

If you want to try to escape out of the hangar, go to 12.

If you wish to surrender, go to 21.

"Give me some information about those ships,"
you order.

The Barracuda obeys.

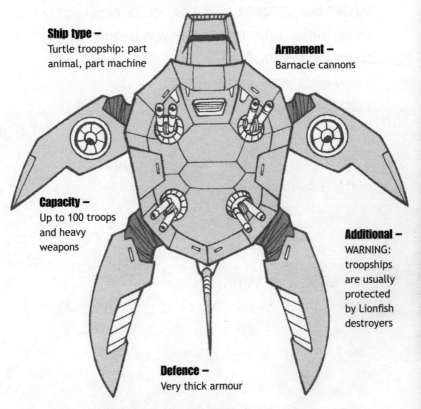

Ship type –
Turtle troopship: part
animal, part machine

Armament –
Barnacle cannons

Capacity –
Up to 100 troops
and heavy
weapons

Additional –
WARNING:
troopships
are usually
protected
by Lionfish
destroyers

Defence –
Very thick armour

To attack the troopships, go to 48.
To search for other vessels, go to 9.
If you wish to retreat, go to 40.

27

You spin the bike around and launch the sub-aqua bike's sea dart missiles. They explode, knocking one of the Atlanteans from his mount. The seahorse hangs in the water undamaged.

The other Atlantean returns fire, but is no match for your weaponry. Another missile finishes off the second enemy.

More vessels stream out of the Man-of-war's hangar. You realise that the attack on the nuclear bases will soon be under way. You will have to move quickly!

If you wish to head to the hangar entrance on your sub-aqua bike, go to 34.

If you wish to ride the cyborg seahorse instead, go to 16.

28

"We'll target the Man-of-war," you say. "If we destroy it, the other ships will retreat and we can follow them."

Shen is not convinced. "There are too many enemy ships here. We should switch to stealth mode and carry out a scouting mission before we attack."

If you wish to take Shen's advice, go to 42.

If you wish to attack the Atlanteans, go to 48.

29

You open fire and take out several of the Atlantean workers. However, one of the remaining Atlanteans hits an alarm. Lights flash and autoguns spring out of the walls and point at you.

Before you can react, they send a stream of poison spines your way. They rip into you. You drop to the floor in silence.

You shouldn't have been so trigger-happy! To begin again, go to 1.

30

"We'll attack the destroyers first and then deal with the troopships," you tell Shen.

"Engaging enemy!" The first Lionfish destroyer doesn't stand a chance as your torpedoes strike. It lights up the dark sea as it explodes. The second destroyer launches its own torpedoes, but you move round and avoid them. Now you are right behind the Lionfish.

"Activate water cannon!" you tell Shen. She punches a button. The super-heated jet cuts into the engines of the Lionfish, setting off a huge fireball which blows the front off the ship.

"Now for the troopships," you say.

"Hold on," interrupts Shen. "Maybe those troopships are heading towards the rest of the

Atlantean fleet. We could attach a tracking device to their shells and see where they are going. It might help us locate the other Atlantean command ships."

You think about Shen's suggestion.

If you wish to attack the troopships as planned, go to 6.

If you want to attach a tracking device onto the enemy ships, go to 13.

31

"We have to let ORCA know," you decide. "Deactivate stealth mode."

The Barracuda obeys. Before you can contact ORCA, the radar screens show a wave of torpedoes heading your way.

"They know we're here!" warns Shen.

"Evasive action and engage enemy!" You spin the Barracuda away from the deadly torpedoes and return fire. You knock out several enemy ships, but for every one you destroy, another ten take its place.

To continue the fight, go to 35.

If you want to retreat, go to 3.

32

You locate the control room on the seahorse's map system. You leave your seahorse on the other side of the airlock, and make your way through the corridors. You are soon at the control room doors. They are guarded by several Atlanteans, carrying harpoon guns and electro-lances.

Suddenly the whole corridor is filled with a high-pitched wailing sound. The Atlanteans know you are here! Before you can react, the guards see you, raise their weapons and signal you to surrender.

If you wish to retreat, go to 12.
If you want to attack the guards, go to 41.
If you decide to surrender, go to 21.

33

Some hours later you are back on board ORCA's submarine headquarters for a briefing.

"While you were testing the Barracuda, we received this message," says Admiral Crabbe.

A 3-D image of Triton fills the screen. "Humankind! You may have stopped my forces from gaining your missiles, but no matter! As I speak, my troops are gathering for an all-out assault on your world! Commander Hadal will lead them to victory. Soon the human race will be destroyed. You have been warned!"

The picture fades away.

"Where are they gathering?" you ask.

"We don't know," replies the admiral. "The Mer have still not been able to find the hole in the seabed and we have had no reported sightings. We're in the dark. They could attack anywhere…"

If you destroyed the Turtle troopships, go to 15.

If you didn't, go to 46.

34

As you approach the Man-of-war's hangar you are caught in a beam of light. The light stays focused on you as you head towards the entrance. Scanners on the wall turn red as you enter the hangar.

Suddenly, an alarm begins to sound out. Panels in the Man-of-war's hull open up to reveal dozens of deadly autocannon batteries pointing at you! A troop of Atlantean guards appear, mounted on cyborg seahorses. They move towards you.

If you want to retreat, go to 12.

If you wish to head inside the ship, go to 25.

35

You continue to fight, but more and more Atlantean ships join in the battle.

"This is madness!" says Shen. "There are too many ships!"

It is the last thing you hear as a torpedo strikes and the Barracuda explodes, sending you and Shen to oblivion.

Learn from your mistakes and go back to 1.

36

You shake your head. "I can't take the risk," you say.

Shen is furious. "Do you really think I'd tell you it's safe if it wasn't? It's my life on the line here as well. If you don't trust me, then it's the end of our partnership."

The Barracuda continues to blast out its warning.

If you want to change your mind, go to 17.

If you want to return to the surface, go to 44.

37

Hadal's shark opens fire, sending a torrent of razor darts your way. You spin and avoid them, but the Atlantean commander follows you and opens fire again.

You counter the attack and fire a sea dart missile. It explodes, but Hadal is not damaged. He rides through the cloud of bubbles and strikes you with his electro-lance. You are blasted through the water.

As you float downwards you see the jaws of Hadal's shark open once more before snapping shut on your body.

You helped to destroy the Man-of-war, but have paid the ultimate price. To begin again, go to 1.

38

"We need to know more about this Man-of-war," you say to Shen. "Barracuda, give us everything you've got on it."

Ship type –
Cyborg Man-of-war —
mother ship control
centre

Capacity –
Up to 1,000 vehicles,
including Crab tanks;
launch bays for Ray
fighters and 10,000+
troops and heavy
weapons

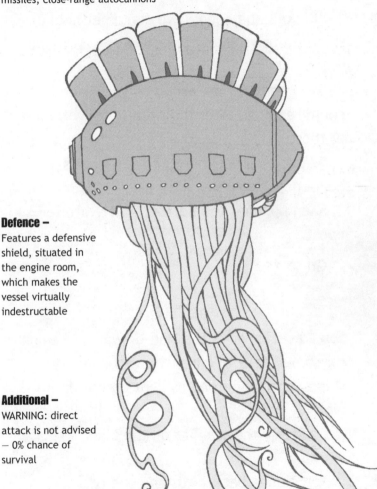

Armaments–
SMART torpedo systems; sea-to-surface
missiles; close-range autocannons

Defence –
Features a defensive
shield, situated in
the engine room,
which makes the
vessel virtually
indestructable

Additional –
WARNING: direct
attack is not advised
– 0% chance of
survival

"We will have to neutralise the defensive shield if we are going to destroy the Man-of-war," says Shen.

"It would be good if we could get hold of that defensive shield to add to the Barracuda," you reply.

Shen nods. "That would be very useful. We could really go after the Atlanteans with one of those."

"Well, let's get there and see what's happening," you say.

Shen punches the button to activate jet boost.

Go to 11.

39

You travel towards the Man-of-war, searching for somewhere to enter the vast ship. The ship's searchlight beams light up the dark waters.

Suddenly the scanner on the bike bleeps a warning.

You glance backwards and see two Atlanteans, mounted on cyborg seahorses, heading towards you! They are carrying deadly electro-lances.

One of the Atlanteans shoots a metal chain lasso at you. You manage to spin the bike around and avoid the coil. The other rider charges towards you with his electro-lance held out.

To attack the Atlanteans, go to 27.
To try to outrun them, go to 7.

40

"Let sleeping turtles lie," you say. "Let's get back to HQ."

As you turn the Barracuda around, an explosion rocks the super sub.

"Incoming torpedoes!" Shen warns. "Two Lionfish destroyers are closing in."

"Deploy countermeasures," you order just in time as another torpedo targets the Barracuda.

If you want to attack the destroyers, go to 30.

To try to escape from your attackers, go to 22.

41

You fire at the enemy with your jet gun. You take out a couple of the Atlanteans, but you are outnumbered. More guards appear. They return fire.

The air is filled with steel darts and harpoon bolts. You manage to dodge the deadly projectiles, but you know you cannot win.

If you wish to try and get away, go to 12.

If you want to surrender, go to 21.

42

"Let's switch to stealth mode and see what the enemy has for us!"

Shen presses a button and guides the Barracuda towards the enemy fleet. Destroyers, troopships and other battle vessels surround the Man-of-war.

As you scan the scene, the Man-of-war's engines suddenly burst into life. It begins to rise up from the ocean floor.

"It's leaving!" says Shen. "It must be heading off to begin the attack."

If you wish to attack the Man-of-war, go to 18.

If you wish to follow it, go to 4.

43

Some time later you wake up. You are in the Man-of-war's control room. Standing before you is a huge figure — it's Commander Hadal!

"Why am I alive?" you ask.

Hadal laughs. "I wanted to show you what is happening to your world."

He flicks a switch and dozens of holographic

images of nuclear explosions fill the room. "Your fellow humans thought they were being attacked by other humans, and now they are fighting each other. Once they have destroyed themselves, we will take over the planet!"

You have failed! The world is at the mercy of the Atlanteans. To begin again, go to 1.

44

"We have to surface," you say, moving the Barracuda upwards.

Shen stares at you before switching on the comms link. "Get me Admiral Crabbe," she says.

Within seconds she is explaining what has happened. Ignoring your protests, Shen says, "I will not work with someone who doesn't trust me. I will return to my people."

"But you and the Mer are vital to ORCA's fight against the Atlanteans," Crabbe says.

"Then you have to decide who you want."

There is a pause before Crabbe replies. "Shen, take over command of the Barracuda and return to HQ."

"What about me?" you say.

"You can return to your unit!"

It is the end of your quest. If you wish to begin again, go to 1.

45

"We need to find the best way into the ship," you tell Shen.

"Scan for the weakest point of entry," you

tell the Barracuda. A hologram of the Man-of-war appears on a screen, along with a report.

- **No entry weak points**
- **The only possible way in is through the hangar door**
- **It is heavily guarded. There is a vehicle identification scanning system.**

- **The chance of successfully boarding is**
3.78 per cent

That's not good, you think. Should you change your plan?

If you wish to attack the Man-of-war, go to 8.

If you still want to try to get on board the Man-of-war, go to 23.

46

"Perhaps the troopships could lead us to the main force," says Shen.

Admiral Crabbe looks puzzled. "What are you talking about?" he asks.

You tell him about the tracking devices you attached to the troopships.

"Well done," says the admiral. "Find out

where those ships are heading."

You link up the Barracuda's tracking system with ORCA's main control room. Soon you have the co-ordinates of where the Atlantean troopships are.

"They aren't moving," Shen points out.

"Then perhaps they've reached their meeting point," you say.

If you wish to head to the meeting point immediately, go to 20.

If you wish to find out more about the troopships' location, go to 24.

47

You head over to the defensive shield control panel. You ignore the engineers as you try to

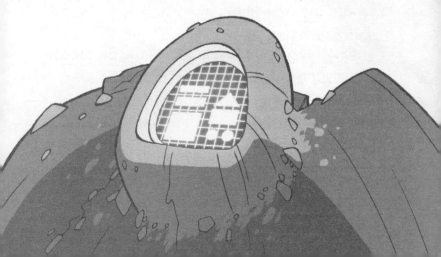

remove the alien-looking device. It is firmly attached, but you manage to prise it away. You have the defensive shield unit!

At that moment, a wailing sound fills the air around you. You quickly head for the door. In the confusion you speed through the corridors, firing at any Atlanteans that get in your way.

As you reach the hangar and leap onto your seahorse, Shen's voice crackles over the comms system. "ORCA attack in two minutes. Are the Man-of-war's defences disabled?"

"Yes," you reply. "Tell Crabbe to attack."

"Are you out yet?"

You look ahead and see the huge hangar entrance doors closing.

"Very nearly..."

Go to 5.

48

"Let's attack," you say, boosting the Barracuda towards the enemy. "Launch torpedoes—"

Suddenly there is a huge explosion at the rear of the Barracuda. You are being attacked!

"Lionfish destroyers!" Shen reports.

Another explosion rocks the Barracuda.
Lights flash and alarms wail.

"Launch countermeasures! Taking evasive
action!" But the Barracuda is hit again by the
Atlantean destroyers.

"Pressure shield generator failing!" cries Shen.

It is the last thing you hear as the Barracuda
is split apart.

**Time to calm down and start your quest
again at 1.**

49

"We'll stay in stealth mode," you decide. "That
way we'll be able to get closer to the Man-of-
war and spring a surprise attack. Then we can
inform ORCA of our position."

Shen nods in agreement.

You carefully guide the Barracuda through
the Atlantean fleet until you are within range
of the Man-of-war.

"So what's the plan?" Shen asks.

**If you know about the Man-of-war's
defences, go to 2.**

If you don't, go to 8.

Some time later you wake up. You are back on board the Barracuda.

"Well done," says Shen. "You decided to have a little nap, so I thought I'd get you back on board."

"You said it would sting a bit, not knock me flying! Well, at least we're both alive. That defensive shield is certainly powerful," you say.

"It's already installed itself into the Barracuda's control panel," says Shen.

"What happened to Hadal?" you ask.

"I fed him to the fishes," replies Shen. "I don't think Triton is going to be very happy with us."

The comms link opens. Admiral Crabbe appears on the screen.

"Well done, you two," smiles the admiral. "The Atlantean ships have fled or surrendered. Looks like we've got them on the run."

"So, we win?" you ask.

The admiral shakes his head. "We've won the battle, but not the war. We still haven't

found the hole in the seabed. We have to push the Atlanteans back to Atlantis and seal up the hole."

You've done well so far, but your job's not over. You've still got work to do if the planet is going to be safe!

TOP SECRET: Barracuda – sub-aqua bike

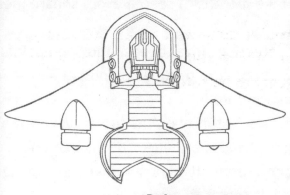

Design –
Intended for short-range travel. Hard for enemies to detect it on scanners because of its streamlined shape.

Armament –
Sea dart missiles

You stare at the Barracuda's scanner screen. "There's a lot of ocean floor down there. It will take months to search every square metre of it."

A detection signal beeps, and Shen points at her screen. "I'm picking up another sub — an Atlantean ship."

You are instantly on the alert. "A warship?"

Shen shakes her head. "No, it looks like a supply vessel. It's leaking fuel and moving slowly. It seems to be damaged."

You give her a grin. "It will be heading home for repairs. All we have to do is follow it..."

Continue the adventure in:

ATLANTIS QUEST 3

BATTLE FOR THE SEAS

I HERO
DECIDE YOUR OWN DESTINY
ATLANTIS QUEST
BATTLE FOR THE SEAS
EDGE
Steve Barlow - Steve Skidmore

About the 2Steves

"The 2Steves" are
Britain's most popular
writing double act
for young people,
specialising in comedy
and adventure. They
perform regularly in schools and libraries,
and at festivals, taking the power of words
and story to audiences of all ages.

Together they have written many books,
including the *Crime Team* and *iHorror* series.

About the illustrator: Jack Lawrence

Jack Lawrence is a successful freelance
comics illustrator, working on titles such as
A.T.O.M., Cartoon Network, *Doctor Who
Adventures*, *2000 AD*, *Gogos Mega Metropolis*
and *Spider-Man Tower of Power*. He also works
as a freelance toy designer.

Jack lives in Maidstone in Kent with
his partner and two cats.

Have you completed the other I HERO Quests?

Battle with aliens in Tyranno Quest:

AIR BLAST

978 1 4451 0875 9 pb
978 1 4451 1345 6 ebook

FIRE STORM

978 1 4451 0876 6 pb
978 1 4451 1346 3 ebook

ICE STRIKE

978 1 4451 0877 3 pb
978 1 4451 1347 0 ebook

EARTH ATTACK

978 1 4451 0878 0 pb
978 1 4451 1348 7 ebook

Defeat the Red Queen in Blood Crown Quest:

SANDS OF BLOOD

978 1 4451 1499 6 pb
978 1 4451 1503 0 ebook

DRAGON MOUNTAIN

978 1 4451 1500 9 pb
978 1 4451 1504 7 ebook

DEMON SEA

978 1 4451 1501 6 pb
978 1 4451 1505 4 ebook

CITY OF THE DEAD

978 1 4451 1502 3 pb
978 1 4451 1506 1 ebook

Also by the 2Steves...

978 0 7496 9283 4 pb
978 1 4451 0843 8 eBook

A millionaire is found at his luxury island home – dead! But no one can work out how he died. You must get to Skull Island and solve the mystery before his killer escapes.

978 0 7496 9284 1 pb
978 1 4451 0844 5 eBook

The daughter of a Hong Kong businessman has been kidnapped. You must find her, but who took her and why? You must crack the case, before it's too late!

978 0 7496 9286 5 pb
978 1 4451 0845 2 eBook

You must solve the clues to stop a terrorist attack in London. But who is planning the attack, and when will it take place? It's a race against time!

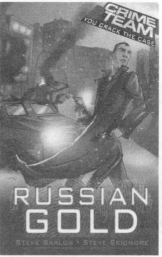

978 0 7496 9285 8 pb
978 1 4451 0846 9 eBook

An armoured convoy has been attacked in Moscow and hundreds of gold bars stolen. But who was behind the raid, and where is the gold? Get the clues - get the gold.